DOG LOVES COUNTING

LOUISE YATES

Alfred A. Knopf
NEW YORK

For Owen

Also by Louise Yates
Dog Loves Books
Dog Loves Drawing

THIS IS A BORZOI BOOK PUBLISHED BY ALFRED A. KNOPF

Copyright © 2013 by Louise Yates

All rights reserved. Published in the United States by Alfred A. Knopf, an imprint of Random House Children's Books, a division of Random House, Inc., New York.

Originally published in hardcover in Great Britain by Jonathan Cape, a division of the Random House Group Ltd., London, in 2013.

Knopf, Borzoi Books, and the colophon are registered trademarks of Random House, Inc.

Visit us on the Web! randomhouse.com/kids

Educators and librarians, for a variety of teaching tools, visit us at RHTeachersLibrarians.com

Library of Congress Cataloging-in-Publication Data

Yates, Louise, author, illustrator.

Dog loves counting / Louise Yates. — First American edition.

p.   cm.

Summary: "Dog loves his books so much that he can't put them down long enough to go to bed! His friends help him count his way to sleep."—

Provided by publisher.

ISBN 978-0-449-81342-3 (trade) — ISBN 978-0-449-81343-0 (lib. bdg.) — ISBN 978-0-449-81344-7 (ebook)

[1. Dogs—Fiction. 2. Bedtime—Fiction. 3. Books and reading—Fiction. 4. Counting—Fiction. 5. Animals—Fiction.] I. Title.

PZ7.Y276Dod 2013

[E]—dc23

2012043219

The text of this book is set in 23-point Century.

The illustrations were created using watercolors.

MANUFACTURED IN CHINA

September 2013

10 9 8 7 6 5 4 3 2 1

First American Edition

Dog loved books. He loved reading
them late into the night and didn't like
to leave them for long.

He knew he must sleep, but Dog just couldn't drift off. He tried counting sheep, but they weren't helping at all.

"Perhaps there are other creatures I could count?" he thought.

Dog reached for a book and began.

The first thing Dog found was an egg.

"One," he counted, and the egg began to hatch.

Inside was a baby dodo.
"Hello, little one," said Dog.
He looked around, but
the dodo was
all alone.

N.°2
Dog

N.°1
The Dodo

"I'll look after you," said Dog. "Together
we are two. Number One, follow me—
we must find Number Three."

They looked on through the book for
the next creature they could count.
"Number Three?" Dog called out.

"Are you speaking to
me?" said a sloth
after a long silence.
He waved very, very slowly.

N°3
The
Three-Toed
Sloth

Dog counted his claws.

The three-toed sloth wanted to help them find more numbers. He took his time, but together they continued on, keeping count all the way.

1... 2...3...

1... 2...3...

1... 2...3...

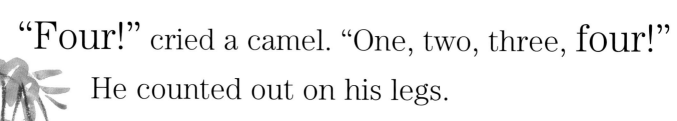

"Four!" cried a camel. "One, two, three, four!"
He counted out on his legs.
"We are counting," explained Dog,
"so that I can fall asleep."

The camel hoped he could help. "In the desert where I come from, there are many more things we can count. Follow me!"

Nº4
The Camel

1

2   3   4

"The next number is five," said the camel. "There is a lizard, I think, called a five-lined skink."

They found him under a log.

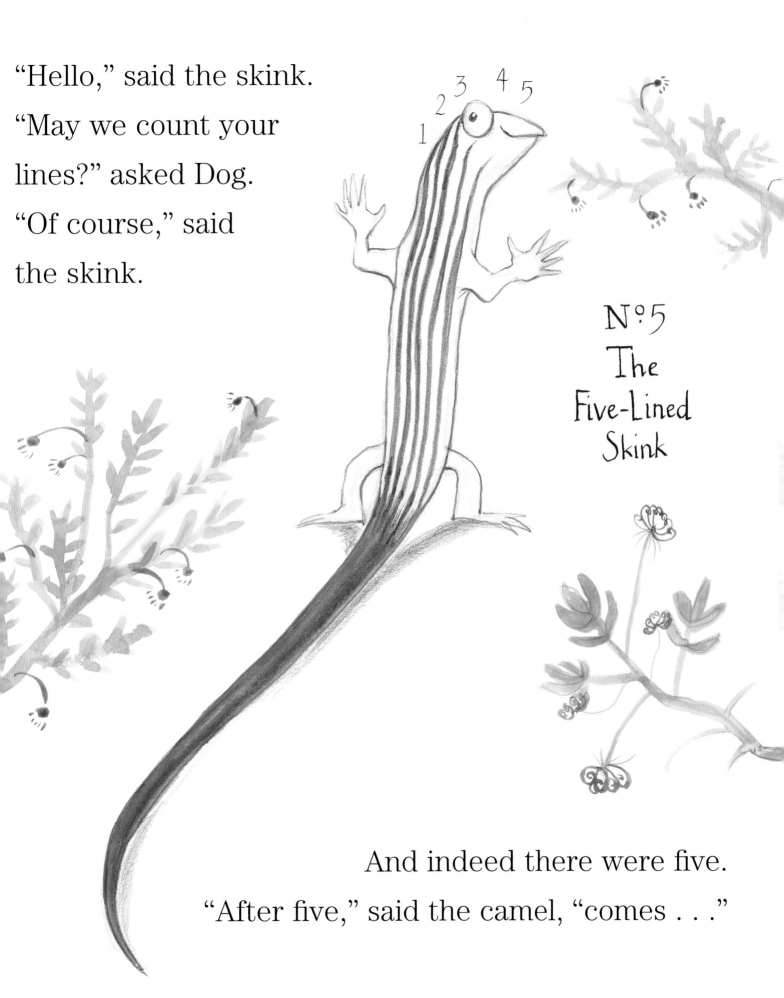

"Hello," said the skink.
"May we count your lines?" asked Dog.
"Of course," said the skink.

N° 5
The Five-Lined Skink

And indeed there were five.
"After five," said the camel, "comes . . ."

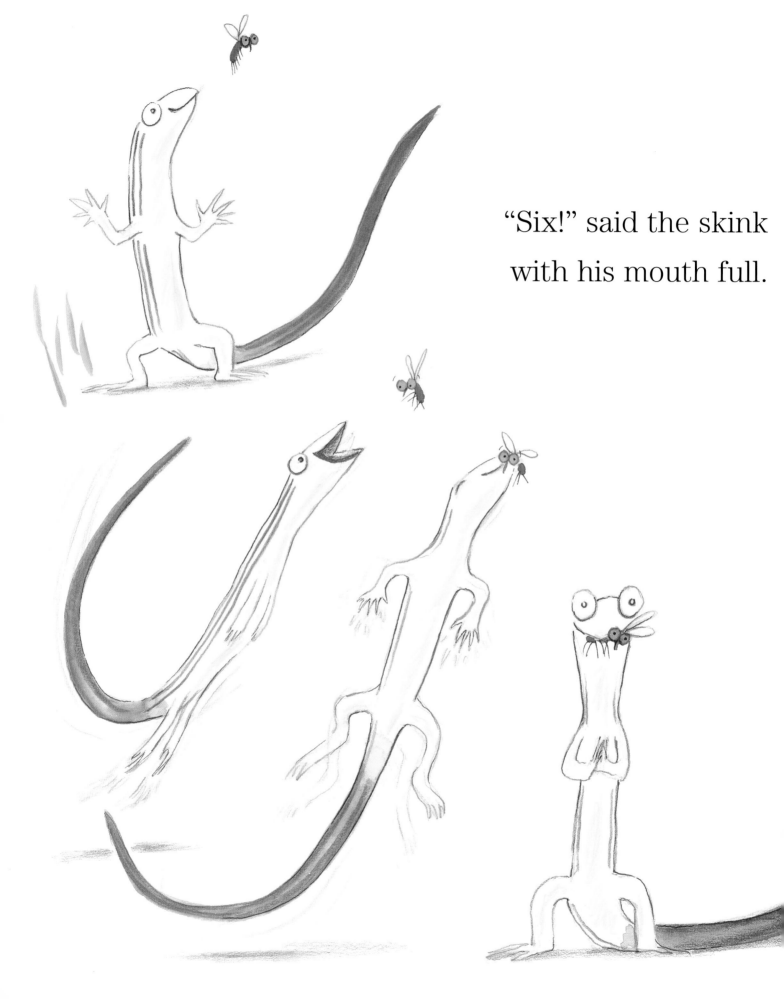

"Six!" said the skink
with his mouth full.

And as he untangled the fly, they quickly saw why.

1 2 3 4 5 6

Nº6
The Fly

"Coooo-eeee!" called a . . .

... raccoon, waving her tail.

She had seven black stripes.

N°7
The Raccoon

1 2

3

4

5   6   7

"We're on our way to the desert," said Dog.

"Can I come too?" called a spider. "Or am I too late?"

1   2   3   4   5   6   7   8

Nº8
The Spider

"Just in time," replied Dog, and they counted to eight.

Number Nine was harder to find—

he was dozing in his burrow.

"Who's in there?" called Dog.

"A nine-banded armadillo," said a voice.

Nº9
The Nine-Banded
Armadillo

123456789

And when the creature came out, they saw it was true.

He joined them too.

"Nearly there," said the camel.

"What number's next?" asked the armadillo.

"Ten!" called a crab, and he scuttled about, waving each leg in turn.

Nº 10
The Crab

1

2

3

4

5

6

7

8

9

10

Dog was enjoying himself!
He couldn't wait to know
more numbers.

But when at last they did reach the desert, Dog was disappointed. There was nothing to count as far as he could see.

"Don't worry," said the camel. "There are as many numbers here as there are grains of sand beneath our feet."

"Let's all count together," said Dog cheerfully.
"Number One . . . ," he began.

But Number One was nowhere to be seen!

"We've lost One!"
cried Dog.
"We must find him!"

They were all
very worried.

So they split up and set off, searching in different directions.

There were ten,
10

then nine,
9

then eight, 8

then seven,
7

then six, 6

then five,
5

then four,
4

then three,
3

then two,
2

and then . . .

. . . there was One.

He was looking up at the stars.
They all joined him, counting up and up,
higher and higher and higher.

Dog loves counting!

"I could do this forever," he said
happily. The others agreed.

When Dog woke up the next morning and looked
at his books, he knew that friends and adventures
were never far away–that was something
he could count on.